*For all the kids who have a dream,*
*and to Kirsten Hall for believing in me, xo*

All rights reserved. Published by Scholastic Press, an imprint of Scholastic Inc., *Publishers since 1920.*
SCHOLASTIC, SCHOLASTIC PRESS, and associated logos are trademarks
and/or registered trademarks of Scholastic Inc.

The publisher does not have any control over and does not assume any responsibility
for author or third-party websites or their content.

Library of Congress Cataloging-in-Publication Data

Names: Gibson, Sabina, author, illustrator.
Title: Unicorn magic / by Sabina Gibson.
Description: First edition. | New York : Scholastic Press, an imprint of Scholastic Inc., 2018. |
Summary: Periwinkle the light-blue unicorn lives in the Forever Forest, but even as she
encourages the other unicorns, she worries that she will never find her own
special magic—until she learns to follow Birdie's advice and believe in herself.
Identifiers: LCCN 2017028690 (print) | ISBN 9780545813310 (jacketed hardcover)
Subjects: LCSH: Unicorns—Juvenile fiction. | Magic—Juvenile fiction. | Self-confidence—Juvenile fiction. |
CYAC: Unicorns—Fiction. | Magic—Fiction. | Self-confidence—Fiction.
Classification: LCC PZ7.1.G53 Un 2018 (print) | DDC [E]—dc23
LC record available at https://lccn.loc.gov/2017028690

10 9 8 7 6 5 4 3 2 1      18 19 20 21 22

Printed in China 62
First edition, July 2018

Book design by Sunny Lee

# Unicorn Magic

## Sabina Gibson

Scholastic Press  •  New York  •  An Imprint of Scholastic Inc.

**Periwinkle** lived in the Forever Forest with her unicorn friends. Every unicorn in the land was born with a magical power.

One day, Periwinkle sat on the ground with her friend. "Birdie, I'm feeling sad!" she said. "I don't think I can do anything special."

"I wish I knew my power," sighed
Periwinkle to her friend.

"Cheer up, cheer up!" tweeted Birdie.
"You just need to believe in magic and
follow your heart!"

Early next morning, Periwinkle galloped around Inspiration Grove, where she found Ruby beginning to create the sunrise.

"I can't decide how to finish painting the sky," said Ruby.

"Birdie told me to believe in magic and follow my heart," said Periwinkle. "Maybe it will work for you."

Ruby thought for a moment and then took a deep breath. And she painted a beautiful sky.

"I love it," said Periwinkle, wishing she could discover her own magical power.

Periwinkle and Birdie found Pearl nearby, on the shore of Reflection Lake. A few puffy clouds hung in the sky overhead.

"I'm not sure my cloud-spinning power is very magical today," said Pearl, sounding a little troubled.

Birdie fluttered her wings. Periwinkle smiled
and said, "Believe in magic and follow your heart."

Pearl closed her eyes, and animal clouds billowed and frolicked across the sky.

"I did it!" exclaimed Pearl. "Thank you, thank you!"

Entering Mellow Meadow, Periwinkle and Birdie saw their friend Marigold.

"I can't decide where to plant the pretty orange and pink flowers," sighed Marigold.

"Don't think about it, and just follow your heart," Periwinkle suggested as her horn gave off small, colorful sparks.

Marigold closed her eyes, and the center of
the meadow filled with sweet-smelling orange
and pink flowers that grew and bloomed.
"Lovely!" exclaimed Marigold.

Periwinkle stopped for a moment.

"Birdie," she sniffled, shedding a few tears.

"What if I don't have any magic in my horn?"

"Nonsense," chirped Birdie. "You are the most magical unicorn I know."

"But, Birdie," said Periwinkle, "Ruby can paint the sky, Pearl can spin animal clouds, and Marigold grows sweet-smelling flowers. I can't do anything magical."

Just then Pearl, Ruby, and Marigold appeared.

"We wanted to thank you for being such a great friend," they chimed.

Periwinkle smiled and joined her friends.
She whispered to them, "I wish I knew my
magical powers."

They all cheered, "Believe in magic and
follow your heart!"

Periwinkle closed her eyes. Her unicorn horn glowed with magic. A beautiful rainbow arched all the way across the forest.

"My magic!" exclaimed Periwinkle.

"We just needed to believe in ourselves," they cheered. "That's the very best magic of all."